Original Korean text by Seon-woong Shin
Illustrations by Eun-yeong Choi

This English edition published by big & SMALL in 2018
by arrangement with Dawoolim
English text edited by Joy Cowley

ISBN: 978-1-925235-33-3
Printed in Korea

What a Beautiful World!

Written by Seon-woong Shin
Illustrated by Eun-yeong Choi
Edited by Joy Cowley

Turn each page to go down, down, down, into our beautiful world.

The bright sun shines
on the planets in our solar system,
including Earth.

Earth orbits the sun every 365 days.
It is day on the side of Earth that faces the sun.

Satellites take pictures of the stars and planets in space.

Outer space turns into our sky.
High above the clouds,
aeroplanes fly.

White clouds drift by
the mountaintop.
Go down the mountain
and the air gets warmer.

Tough evergreen trees grow in the cool mountain air.

Birds and animals
live in the forest.
Beneath the mountain
is a calm lake.

On the ground, plants grow
and people live near a river.
All kinds of animals scurry,
run and jump.

In the dark underground,
small animals dig tunnels and burrows.
Fossils from long ago are buried below.

 Now close this book and turn it over to travel from outer space to deep undersea.

What a Beautiful World!

There are many layers of our beautiful world. See what it is like from outer space down through the sky and deep into the ground. Then see what is below Earth's oceans. Our planet is filled with life.

Let's think!

How long does it take for the moon to orbit Earth?

What kinds of trees grow on cold mountains?

What do animals dig in the ground?

Where do coral reefs form?

Let's do!

Take a look at what's in soil. Dig out a cup of soil. Spread it out on a flat, clean surface. What can you find in the soil? Make a list of what you find. Draw pictures too. Do you see part of leaves? Do you see sand or rocks? Did you find any insects?

Earth's Soil

Below Earth's surface is soil. It has layers too. In the top layers, animals and insects dig tunnels. Plant roots grow down. Dead leaves and animals break down. They make the soil rich with nutrients. The soil below contains clay, sand, and minerals. Even deeper, the soil gets rocky.

Oceans

The deep ocean is filled with life. Near the top, the water is warmer. It gets more sunlight. Plants grow well in this layer. Many animals live there too. Below this is the Twilight Zone. It is darker in this layer. Plants cannot live there. Animals have big eyes. Some animals make their own light. Further down is the Midnight Zone. It is very dark and cold in this layer. Much less life is in this layer.

Layers of Our World

Earth has many layers. Gases wrap around the planet as the atmosphere. Earth's surface has rivers, mountains and other natural features. Below the surface, soil and rock lead to the center of our world.

The Atmosphere

Earth's atmosphere has five layers. The closest layer is where weather happens. It traps heat by Earth's surface. It is rich with the oxygen we need to breathe. All the layers protect us from harmful rays from outer space.

Earth's Surface

There are many kinds of landforms on Earth's surface. Mountains rise high. The tallest go higher than 26,000 feet (8,000 metres). Deep canyons cut into the surface. Wide grassy plains are home to many animals, like zebras and bison. Oceans, rivers and streams cover the surface with water. Many animals and people live on Earth's surface.

Even the bottom of the sea
is filled with wonder and beauty.
Strange creatures glow in the dark water.
What a beautiful world!

Some animals create light from chemicals
in their bodies.

Whales are some of the biggest ocean creatures.
The blue whale is the biggest creature on Earth.

Under the sea, fish, mammals
and many other creatures swim.
They search for food.

A coral reef forms in warm tropical water.
It is home to many creatures.

People have fun
on the sandy shore.

In the middle of the sea
is an island.

Below the clouds, the seabirds fly over the ocean and a big ship during the day.

In the night sky,
aeroplanes fly with
their lights on.

Stars shine brightly.

The moon orbits Earth every 27 days.

Turn each page to go down into the sea.

Near Earth is the moon
with its many craters.
It reflects light from the sun.